This book belongs to:

....

....

....

For Little Bear—F. H.
For William and Edward—S. H.

little bee books

An imprint of Bonnier Publishing Group
853 Broadway, New York, NY 10003
Text copyright © 2014 by Felix Hayes
Illustrations copyright © 2014 by Sue Heap
First published in Great Britain by Templar Publishing.
This little bee books edition, 2015.
All rights reserved, including the right of reproduction in whole or in part in any form.
LITTLE BEE BOOKS is a trademark of Bonnier Publishing Group, and associated colophon
is a trademark of Bonnier Publishing Group.
Manufactured in China 0315 008
First Edition 2 4 6 8 10 9 7 5 3 1
Library of Congress Control Number: 2014958644
ISBN 978-1-4998-0077-7

www.littlebeebooks.com
www.bonnierpublishing.com

George
and the
Dinosaur

by
Felix Hayes

illustrated by
Sue Heap

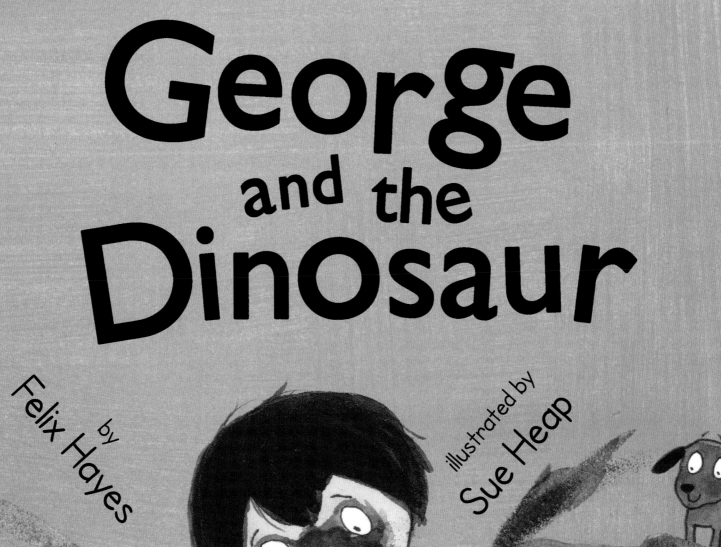

This is
George.

George
loves
digging.

So far he has found . . .

some gems,

a sword,

a pirate's peg leg,

and,

to top it all off,

a **dinosaur egg!**

But,

when he cleans
his treasure,
he finds . . .

the gems
are stones, dirt,
and dust.

The sword
is a spoon,
all covered
in rust.

The leg is a root,
cracked and dried.

But the egg's still an egg
with **something** inside!

George puts
the egg in the
cupboard under
the stairs.

George checks the egg every day.

On the first day he hears a
tap, tap, tap.

A few days later he spies
a crack.

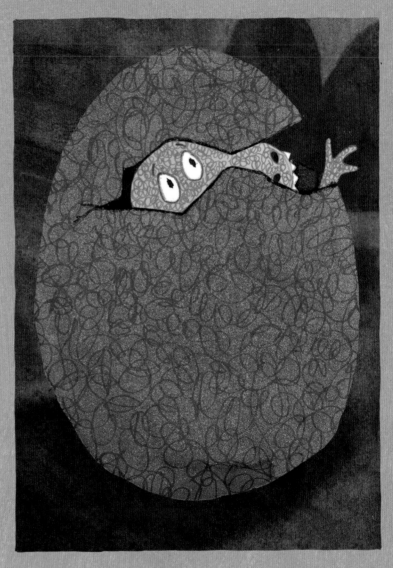

Then, when the egg starts to rumble and shake . . .

Oops, thinks George. *Have I made a mistake?*

But after a week
he opens the door . . .

and there it is—

HIS DINOSAUR!

With fins down its back and lots of teeth,
it is green on top and yellow beneath.

With just one look,
George is sure:
This is no ordinary
dinosaur.

It looks around.

"Mommy?"

it says.

"Er ...Yes?"
says George
and pats its head.

George thinks
his dinosaur is
perfect.

my dinosaur is perfect.

The dinosaur looks hungry,
so George gives it his lunch.

He gives it . . .

an apple, a sandwich,

some chopped-up carrot,

and a delicious biscuit

in the shape

of a parrot.

But his

dinosaur

still looks

hungry.

So George takes his dinosaur into the kitchen.

When he opens the fridge, on comes the light, and his dinosaur **eats...**

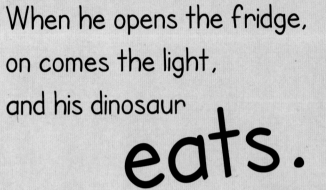

mom
my
dinosaur
was
hungry!

ABC

Pizza

everything
in sight:

the milk, the cheese,
some chocolate mousse—
all washed down
with pineapple juice.
It even eats mold
from a jar at the back.
But all of this food
is only a snack.

His dinosaur
still looks
hungry!

milk

So George finds it some more things to eat.

It eats all the plates
from the cupboard downstairs,
the towels from the bathroom,
the table and chairs.

It gobbles down books
and a tangerine,
the fridge, the TV,
and the washing machine,

a tree from
the garden,
the paddling pool . . .

and Class 2's mouse George
brought home from school.

(George
never liked
the mouse
much, so
he doesn't
mind.)

George thinks his dinosaur HAS to
be full by now.

But the dinosaur smiles a wicked grin,
and opens its mouth to stuff more in.
Mom's best dress, the lamp from the hall,
the dog, its leash, and its red squeaky ball.

Even Mom and Dad
are just a bite
for a
greedy
dinosaur's
appetite!

The dinosaur

scoops up George
and sets off into
town . . .

On the way it eats everything it sees:
a postman, a cow, a hive of bees,

two sweet old ladies having a chat.
And with every bite, it just gets fat.

A car, a truck, a tractor, a bus
are all gobbled down without any fuss.

George's dinosaur

eats

everything.

And I mean
EVERYTHING!

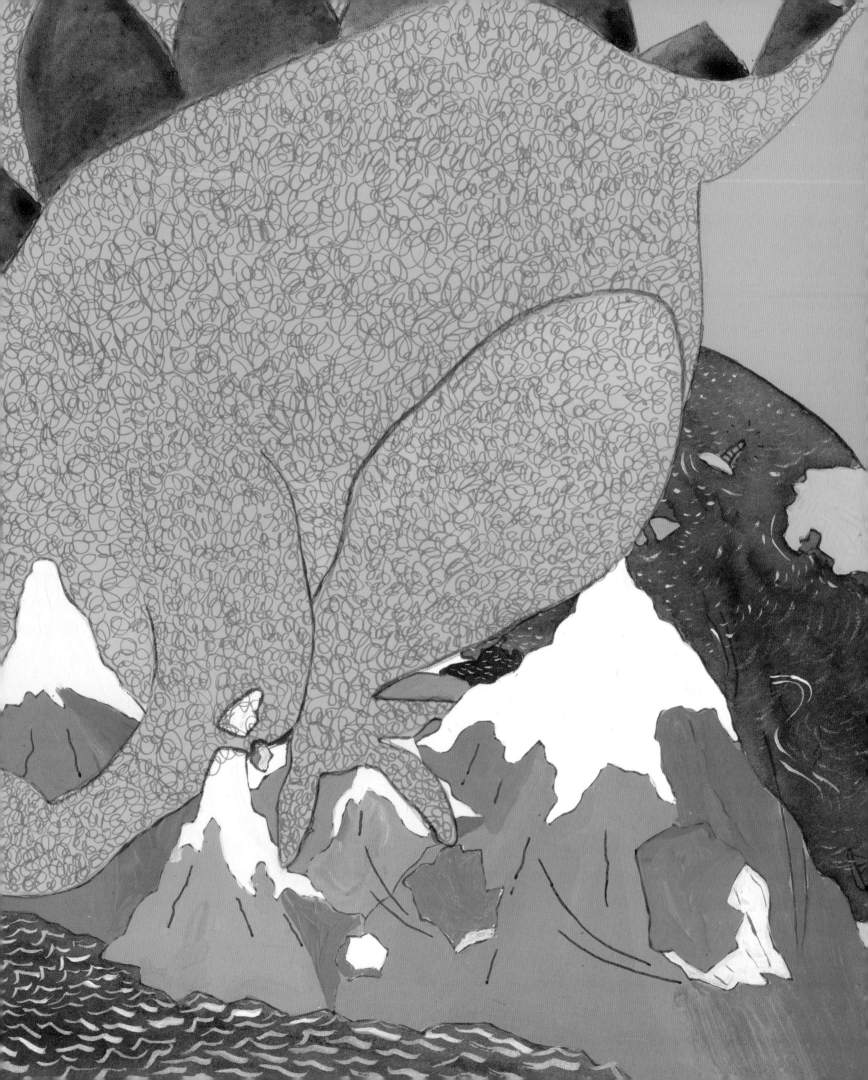

Finally, nothing is left . . .

nothing at all.

Not a bean, not a mouse.

Nothing except . . .

George.

George looks at the dinosaur,

the dinosaur

looks at him,

opens

its

terrible jaws

and . . .

pops him in!

Then something starts to happen.

The dinosaur's tummy begins to bubble and squeak.

Its guts first gurgle and then they creak.

Its belly starts to rumble, and then to quake.

Oops!

it thinks, *I've made*

a mistake!

Its tummy swells

as it slobbers and slurps,

then the greedy dinosaur

finally . . .

URPS

Out fly all of
the things it's eaten:
the cars, the buildings,
the people, and even
all of the things
from George's house—
his mom, his dad,
the dog,
and the mouse.

And last of all . . .

. . . George!

"Well, that was fun!"
he says.

He dusts himself off and gets to his feet.

"Do we still need to find
you things to eat?"

The dinosaur looks sheepish
and shakes its head.

"Then pick up that spade
and let's **DIG** instead!"

I wonder what they will find next. . . .